Junkyard Dan

Mercy

NOX PRESS
books for that extra kick to give you more power
www.NoxPress.com

Also by Elise Leonard:

The **JUNKYARD DAN** series: (***Nox Press***)
1. Start of a New Dan
2. Dried Blood
3. Stolen?
4. Gun in the Back
5. Plans
6. Money for Nothing
7. Stuffed Animal
8. Poison, Anyone?
9. A Picture Tells a Thousand Dollars
10. Wrapped Up
11. Finished
12. Bloody Knife
13. Taking Names and Kicking Assets
14. Mercy

THE SMITH BROTHERS (a series): (***Nox Press***)
1. All for One
2. When in Rome
3. Get a Clue
4. The Hard Way
5. Master Plan

A LEEG OF HIS OWN (a series): (***Nox Press***)
1. Croaking Bullfrogs, Hidden Robbers
2. 20,000 LEEGS Under the C
3. Failure to Lunch
4. Hamlette

The **AL'S WORLD** series: (***Simon & Schuster***)
Book 1: Monday Morning Blitz
Book 2: Killer Lunch Lady
Book 3: Scared Stiff
Book 4: Monkey Business

The **LEADER** series: (***Nox Press***)
- ★ Honor
- ★ Courage
- ★ Respect
- ★ Service
- ★ Integrity
- ★ Commitment
- ★ Loyalty
- ★ Duty

PETE'S PLACE (a series): (***Nox Press***)
1. On Ice
2. Coffee to Go

Junkyard Dan

Mercy

Elise Leonard

NOX PRESS
books for that extra kick to give you power
www.NoxPress.com

Leonard, Elise
Junkyard Dan series / Mercy
ISBN: 978-1-935366-07-2

Copyright © 2010 by Elise Leonard.
All rights reserved, including the right of reproduction in whole or in part in any form. Published by Nox Press.
www.NoxPress.com

First Nox Press printing: September 2010

For those who struggle with reading,
I hope my books will help you strengthen
your reading muscles.

Those who know me know that I *always* say:
"If you want to learn how to read...
you actually have to **read**!
It's the same with sports and playing an instrument.
All the lessons and coaching are fine and dandy,
but if you don't pick up a ball or play the instrument,
you're never going to improve!"

I applaud all of the learners who have decided to
strengthen their reading muscles!
And I thank you for reading my books.
I hope you continue to enjoy them.

There are *many* wonderful schools and adult literacy
programs throughout the United States.
Some of which I have already noted in dedications in
my books.

But I would like to dedicate *this* book to
Literacy Partners of Kewaunee County, Wisconsin

Your dedication to literacy is noteworthy!
(I say that because I think you actually have more
tutors in your county than cows.
And your county has a *heck* of a lot of cows!)

This book is also dedicated to a cool bunch of guys:
Bob Garfinkel, **Ken Brydon** and **Mike Urmanski**.
(You guys know what you did to earn my respect.)

~Elise

Chapter 1

I rented a truck.

Then I started driving it to Rosa.

The sooner I got there, the sooner Rosa would come back to Peaceville.

So I tried to drive fast. But the truck wouldn't let me.

I couldn't get the stupid truck to go past 50 miles per hour.

I was so frustrated.

It was like torture.

I was so close, and yet, so far.

By "so close" I didn't mean physically.

Elise Leonard

Rosa was still far away.

And with the way this truck was driving, it will take many hours to get there.

I meant "so close" in that Rosa was coming back to Peaceville *much* sooner than I had hoped.

How cool was that?!

Life was finally going my way for once.

Not that I think life should always go my way.

It was just that things had been hard for me since that day Patti left me.

My whole life had turned upside down.

I didn't know how things would turn out for me.

I didn't know if I would find happiness again.

But I *did*.

That was a shock to me.

Not that I didn't think I deserved it.

I was a good man. Always have been. So of course I thought I deserved to be happy.

But that doesn't mean you always get it.

Sometimes, happiness eludes the nicest people.

Mercy

And sometimes, the worst, most horrible people on this planet get to be happier than pigs in poop.

I never got that.

It just didn't sit well with me.

But it *was* reality.

There was even this book once, titled, "When Bad Things Happen to Good People."

Imagine that! Someone wrote a whole *book* about it!

But I was happy now.

I owned the junkyard. I lived a nice simple life.

I liked where I lived.

Peaceville was the best!

I had good friends. (Even Bubba was a good friend.)

Life was finally good.

I don't know why Patti was back. But I *did* know that I had changed.

I had changed a lot.

She didn't have that control of my emotions

the way she used to.

In fact, I really don't see how I was so head over heels in love with her.

I guess I wasn't really looking at her.

I was seeing her for the person I wanted her to be. Not for the person she was.

But here I was. On my way to get Rosa.

On my way to bring her back to Peaceville.

Life was good.

I was happy.

Until the phone rang.

Chapter 2

"Hey, boss," Bubba said.

"Would you stop calling me that?!" I said.

Bubba laughed.

"Nah," he said. "It's too much fun to tick you off."

"I'm not ticked off. I just don't like when you say that."

"Then you're *really* not going to like what I say next."

I held my breath.

"I don't know how to say this," Bubba said.

This had to be bad.

When was the last time Bubba was at a loss for words?!

This could *not* be good!

"Just tell me," I said.

"Well, it's kind of a funny story," Bubba said.

I rolled my eyes.

"Not 'ha ha' funny. But, I don't know, *weird* funny."

"Spit it out, Bubba."

"Well, you know Patti. Right?"

"Please tell me you didn't ask her out," I said.

"Well, no. I never had the chance."

That was a good thing.

"You know how Hilda hated her?" Bubba asked.

"Hate's a strong word," I said. "But yes, I did know that Hilda took offense at many of the things Patti said and did."

"Well, Patti must have figured that out too."

"And?" I asked.

"And, well, so Patti didn't go back to the diner."

Mercy

"Okay," I said. "I'm sure Hilda is okay with that."

"Hilda's fine with it!" Bubba said.

"So what's the problem?" I asked.

"I'm afraid to tell you," Bubba said.

"Why?" I asked.

"Because you're going to kill me."

Oh *that* did not sound good!

"What did you *do*, Bubba?"

"Well, it's sort of not what I *did*. It's sort of what I *didn't* do."

I was losing patience.

"Okay. So what *didn't* you do, Bubba?!"

"Well, remember when you first moved to Peaceville? *Before* you moved here, really."

"What are you talking about, Bubba?"

"You know. Before you moved here. When you came to my garage that first time."

I *did* remember that.

It felt like ages ago.

I had no idea what he was talking about.

But I did start thinking about my first time in

Bubba's garage.

I got the gas.

I paid for it inside.

I remembered seeing Bubba for the first time.

I remember how I was surprised by him. His black boots and shirt and pants and hair. How his hair was all crazy looking.

I recalled seeing his piercings for the first time. And how I felt that he looked so different than what I had expected.

Then I remembered...

Oh no...

This was *not* good.

It couldn't be.

Please, *please* tell me my thoughts were way off!

Chapter 3

"The vending machine," I said.

"Yup," Bubba said.

"You're kidding me, right?"

"Nope," he said.

I groaned.

"The funny thing is that she picked the *exact* same sandwich you picked."

"The egg salad?!" I screamed.

"Yup," he said.

"I told you to get rid of those sandwiches!" I hollered.

"Everyone knows not to eat them."

Elise Leonard

I sighed.

"Not everyone, Bubba," I said.

"Everyone who counts," Bubba said.

A motorcycle cut me off, then shot me the bird.

Like it was *my* fault the truck could only go 50 miles per hour, max!

"Look, Bubba, I'm driving, and this stupid truck has no pickup and won't go faster than fifty. I can't deal with the whole Patti thing right now. You did stop her from eating that sandwich like you did with me, right?" I asked.

"Well, that's the problem, Dan. I wasn't at the garage when she bought the sandwiches and pigged out on them."

"Sandwiches?" I asked. "More than one?"

"Yeah," Bubba said. "She bought three, and then chowed down on them."

I knew how old those sandwiches were.

"Oh my God," I said.

"Yeah," Bubba said. "I think your pretty wife has an eating disorder."

Mercy

"She's not my wife," I said.

"Officially, she is," Bubba stated. "At least that's what it says on her insurance forms."

Insurance forms were involved, which meant this was a problem.

"How sick is she?" I asked.

I knew she must have gotten food poisoning. How could she not?

"She's in the hospital," Bubba said.

I almost veered off the road.

"The *hospital*?!"

"It's bad, Dan. She's really, *really* sick, and she demanded to see the owner of the garage."

I could just imagine how *that* went over.

I was almost too afraid to ask.

"And what did she do when she saw it was you?"

Bubba scoffed.

"Let's just say... she went ballistic," Bubba said.

"Ballistic as in screaming and yelling?" I asked.

"Well, yeah, she did that. And I have to tell you, Dan, she's mighty good at that."

I had to smile at his comment.

"You don't have to tell *me*," I said. "I know firsthand that she's good at screaming and yelling."

She sure did enough of it while we were married.

"She also did something else, Dan," Bubba said.

I imagined her throwing a vase of flowers at Bubba.

I pictured the vase shattering when it hit the floor.

It was the kind of dramatic thing Patti would do.

"She got a high-powered lawyer," Bubba said. "And she's suing me, the garage and the entire town."

Chapter 4

I think I cursed under my breath.

I thought the vase scenario was overdoing things.

But suing Bubba, the garage and the entire town?! That was the *height* of overdoing things.

I had to hand it to her, though.

She knew Bubba wouldn't have a pot to pee in. So she went after his garage.

She also figured that the garage wasn't worth much, either, so she went for the town.

I wondered if that was her idea or the lawyer's idea.

I also wondered who the lawyer was.

Probably someone from New York.

Bubba had said that he was a "high powered" lawyer.

There weren't too many high-powered lawyers in Peaceville.

Okay, so there probably weren't *any*.

But Rosa was a lawyer, so she might be able to help.

"Let me call Rosa," I said to Bubba. "Meanwhile, stay as far away from Patti as you can."

Bubba said nothing.

"Did you hear me, Bubba?" I asked.

"Yeah," he said. "I heard you."

"Just stay away from her," I repeated.

"But maybe I could charm her to not go through with this lawsuit thing," Bubba said.

"Bubba, no offense, but if you go anywhere *near* her, she'll just get more ticked off."

"But..."

"No, Bubba. Do yourself and the town a favor

Mercy

and *stay away*."

He still said nothing.

"Bubba, you need to trust me on this," I said. "*Do* nothing, *say* nothing, and keep *away* from Patti!"

With that said, I hung up.

I called Rosa.

"Hi, Dan! Where are you?" she said brightly.

I knew I'd smile when I heard her voice. But my smile deepened when I heard how excited she sounded.

"I'm on my way, Rosa," I said. "But the truck is chugging along, so it will take a little bit longer than I expected."

"That's okay," she said. "As long as you get here."

Again, I smiled deeply.

"We seem to have a crisis on our hands," I said.

Rosa gasped.

"What is it?!" she said loudly. "Are you okay?"

"I'm fine. It's Bubba," I said.

"Did he get hurt? Is he okay? What happened?" she shot out quickly.

"He's fine," I said. "It's Patti who got hurt."

"I'm confused," Rosa said.

So I told her the whole story.

Chapter 5

"Keep him away from Patti," Rosa said. "He'll only enrage her further."

"I already told him that," I said.

"Yes," she said. "But will he *do* it?!"

I rolled my eyes. "Who knows?!"

I heard paper rustling.

"Are you packing?" I asked.

"As fast as I can," she said lightly.

That made me laugh.

"Well, I'm on my way," I said. "Don't hurt yourself."

Rosa laughed.

"What does that mean? Do you think I'll get a paper cut from crinkling up the newspaper while I pack my dishes and stuff?"

I had to smile.

"No," I said. "I was talking about moving furniture."

Rosa giggled.

"I'll leave that to you, if you don't mind," she said.

"Good," I replied.

"So how much longer until you get here?" she asked.

"Another four hours or so. It's taking so long because of the truck."

"That's okay," she said. "I'm a packing maniac."

"Are you okay?" I asked.

"What do you mean?" she said.

"You know, leaving your job, your place, and coming back to Peaceville."

"Well," she said slowly. "I don't like the fact that I don't *have* the sheriff's job. And that I might

Mercy

not *get* the sheriff's job. But to be honest, I wanted to come home for a while now. At least I wanted to get away from here. I didn't like my job. It was not what I thought it would be. So I think it's for the best."

I understood how she felt.

I used to feel the same way. But I didn't have a "home" to come home to.

When I was feeling those same feelings, my "home" was with Patti.

But it must feel good for Rosa to have a nice place to return to. With people who love her and care about her.

I know that now that I live in Peaceville, and have good friends, I'd want to return back here.

Those thoughts made me think of Patti.

I thought of my life back in New York.

I was miserable there.

I hated my job. I didn't like the people I worked with.

I *thought* I had friends, but I didn't. They were all Patti's friends. Or people who wanted something from me or felt they could *get* something from me. But they weren't my friends.

Not like my friends now.

Bubba, Hilda, Judge Simpkins, Miles, Henry, Mel and Rosa were *great*!

And I now had Lucky and the rest of the dogs and cats at the yard.

My life was good now.

I was hoping that Rosa felt she was coming towards a better life, too.

"I know Mel will be happy to have you back," I said. "And Hilda, Bubba, Henry, Miles, Judge Simpkins and Lucky will be happy, too!"

Rosa laughed.

"When you mention the gang like that, it makes me *so* happy to be coming home!"

"*I'm* happy that you are coming home, too," I said softly.

"And *that* makes me the happiest of all," she said just as softly.

Just then my phone beeped.

I had another call coming in.

Chapter 6

Of course, it was Patti.

Patti had some sort of radar.

Every time things started to warm up with Rosa, Patti would be right there with a bucket of cold water to ruin the moment.

"Patti's calling," I told Rosa.

"Take it," Rosa said. "Maybe you can calm her down so she doesn't sue Bubba and the town."

I groaned.

"Do it for me," Rosa said.

She was such a great woman.

I was so lucky to have met her, and am even

luckier that she is in my life.

"Okay," I said. "I'll do it for you."

Rosa giggled.

"Just don't be *too* nice to her," Rosa said.

I pretended to be insulted.

"Hey," I said. "What kind of a guy do you think I *am*?! I'm not that kind of guy! *I* don't use my body to get favors from people."

She laughed, just like I wanted her to.

"You could, you know," she flirted.

My grin was so wide, it could have split my face in two.

But then the phone beeped again.

See? There was that cold bucket of water to ruin the moment!

Patti awaited.

I hung up with Rosa and took Patti's call.

"I just heard about your, ah, illness," I said. "Is there anything I can do?"

"Yes," Patti said. "You can help me wipe that idiot off the face of the earth."

"Who, Bubba?"

Mercy

"Yes," Patti said. "And what kind of stupid name is that?! Bubba!"

"It's a southern name that goes back generations—"

"I don't *care* about where the name comes from!" Patti screeched as she interrupted me.

I sighed heavily.

"I just want that idiot wiped off the face of the earth! I ate one of his old sandwiches from his vending machine, and I'm nearly dying!"

"I heard it was three sandwiches," I said.

Patti growled like a lion.

I knew the hard way that that was her way of relieving anger and frustration. *Major* anger and frustration.

But I realized that all of a sudden I had another question for Patti.

"Why didn't you go to Hilda's to eat?" I asked.

"I didn't like the way that woman looked at me."

"Well, you *did* insult her, Patti."

"I never said a *word* to her!"

"You wiped down her seats," I said.

"So?"

"And you wiped down her silverware. In *front* of her!"

"So?"

"So, that's insulting," I said.

I couldn't believe I had to tell her that.

"You know, now that you mention it, Dan, I should sue her too! If it weren't for her attitude, I wouldn't have bought those sandwiches when I bought gas."

"Whoa," I said. "I never said that—"

She cut me off.

"Gotta run. I have to call my lawyer. Thanks, Dan, for the advice."

Then she hung up.

The advice?!

What advice?!

I never gave her any advice.

Chapter 7

I didn't know what to do.

I kept driving as my mind raced.

I think my mind was going faster than the stupid truck.

It sure felt that way.

But I couldn't come up with a good solution.

I couldn't come up with *any* solution.

I'd really tried to think this through. But nothing was coming to mind that would help this situation.

After about an hour of trying to come up with an answer, I called Rosa.

Elise Leonard

"I messed things up further," I said.

"What do you mean?" Rosa asked.

"Now she's suing Hilda, too."

"What?!" Rosa said.

"Patti's suing Hilda. And she somehow thinks that it was *my* idea."

"You would never say to do anything like that," Rosa said.

I was thankful that she knew that.

It made me feel a little better.

But Patti was still going to sue Hilda now, and it was partly my fault.

So I had to *do* something about it all.

But I had no idea *what* I was going to do!

Every time I opened my mouth, things got worse.

"What should I do?" I asked Rosa.

"I have no clue," Rosa said. "Let me think about it for a while, okay?"

"Okay," I said glumly.

"Mel called," Rosa said. "She said that the Vega's are having a party for me when we get back to town."

"That'll be nice," I said.

"I think so," Rosa said. "Want to be my date to the party?"

"I'd love to," I said.

"Three more hours until you're here," Rosa said.

I smiled.

"Three more hours," I repeated. "It feels like a hundred."

"Our time will come," Rosa said softly.

I was hoping it would. And I wasn't talking about just getting there in three hours.

I was hoping our time together would start for real. You know, as a couple.

But first I had to not only get rid of Patti and her lawsuits. But I had to ask her for a divorce.

I wanted to clear the way for me to have a new life. But I knew Patti would not give me up easily.

Not that she wanted me.

She wanted my money.

My old money.

The money she took.

The money she hoped I could work for and replace.

But that wasn't going to happen.

And I was hoping that as soon as Patti realized that, she would gladly give me up.

But she wasn't really getting that through her head right now.

It was like she couldn't wrap her head around the fact that I didn't want that life anymore.

And to be honest, I was a little nervous about what she would do when it *did* finally hit her.

Chapter 8

"Are you still there?" Rosa asked.

"Yes, sorry. I'm still here," I replied.

"Okay," Rosa said. "Well, drive carefully."

"I will," I said.

The rest of the trip went by slowly, but at least I finally got there.

I found Rosa's address easily.

It was parking that was the problem.

It was hard to park a big truck in the city.

I took the boxes and tape from my truck, and walked up to Rosa's apartment.

She swung open the door with great joy.

"You're here! You're here!" she squealed.

That made me feel great. She was so excited to see me.

I was equally excited to see her, but I was glad that she was excited to see me, too.

I looked around her place.

All the pictures were already off the walls. And much of her stuff was already in boxes. But I could tell that it used to look nice.

She had good taste.

Her furniture was nice. It wasn't fancy, but it was practical. And it looked sturdy.

It wasn't all frilly and lacy. Although I had no idea *why*, I was glad to see that.

Patti went for the lacy, frilly, girly stuff, and I was too large a man to be comfortable in that.

I'd always felt as if I were a guest in my own home in New York.

And those white carpets were totally impractical.

I looked at Rosa's carpets. They were darker.

Rosa giggled.

Mercy

"Why are you looking at my carpeting like that?"

"I like it," I said. "Did you pick it out?"

"Yes," she said. "Before I moved in, the landlord had to replace all the carpeting, so he let me pick out the colors."

"Hm," I said, nodding. "And what would you call this color?"

Rosa laughed.

"Maroon."

I nodded.

"Good choice," I said. "And what colors did you choose for the rest of the place?"

"I'll give you the fifty-cent tour," she said lightly.

She grabbed my hand and took me on a tour of her apartment.

"This is the kitchen," she said.

No carpet in there.

It had a plain floor, but she had a nice, small table and two chairs.

"Very nice," I said.

She smiled. "Thanks."

Then she took me to the bedroom.

"And, um, this is my bedroom," she said shyly.

I didn't know why I expected it to be all pink and purple, but it wasn't.

She had not started packing it up yet, so it was fully intact.

It was a beautiful place.

A place of warmth and comfort.

"Wow," I said.

"You like it?" she asked.

"It's amazing," I said.

"It's my comfort place," she said.

I just looked at her.

"My place to come home to and find comfort after a long day."

I nodded.

"I can see what you mean."

Her bed was beautiful.

It was covered in a bedspread with rich colors, and had lots of pillows of different sizes.

Mercy

The colors were great.

It was a mixture of reds and golds and browns and greens.

I know it sounds like it would be drab and ugly, but it was warm and inviting and, well, homey.

"You look tired," Rosa said.

I looked down at Rosa.

"Yes, a little."

"Would you like to take a nap before we get to work?" she asked.

Now that she mentioned it, it was a great idea.

"Sure," I said.

"Well," she said. "Make yourself at home. There are fresh towels in the bathroom."

She pointed to a door on the far side of the room.

"And sleep as long as you'd like. I know you have been on the road a long time."

"Thank you," I said.

She looked a little weird. Like she didn't know what to do next.

So I walked over to her and gently kissed her.

Chapter 9

She smiled up at me before she turned to leave the room.

Then she left the room, so I could sleep.

I hit the bed, and didn't even take off the bedspread.

The moment my head hit one of the many pillows, I was out like a light.

When I woke up, I washed my face and walked out of the bedroom.

Rosa was still packing up her things.

"How'd you sleep?" she asked.

"Like a log," I said with a grin.

Mercy

She smiled.

"Good," she said. "And thanks for the boxes. I was almost out."

We spent the next few hours packing up and loading the truck.

Her stuff fit easily inside.

Once everything was done, I realized I was hungry.

"Do you have a favorite restaurant around here?" I asked.

"There's a great Tex-Mex place around the corner."

Rosa had the shrimp fajitas. The shrimp was grilled with onions and sweet peppers. It was served with rice, refried beans, guacamole and sour cream.

I had three grilled tenderloin medallions served with cheese enchiladas con carne. That came with Spanish rice, guacamole salad and charro bean soup.

It was delicious!

"I can see why you like this place," I said.

"Wait until you try my favorite dessert," Rosa said.

I knew how much she loved chocolate, so I was expecting some sort of chocolate concoction.

Like chocolate cake with chocolate filling and chocolate ice cream. Topped with chocolate syrup and chocolate whipped cream.

Talk about death by chocolate.

But that's not what she ordered.

For dessert we had chocolate caramel nachos. They were delicious, crispy cinnamon-sugar chips topped with vanilla ice cream and drizzled with caramel and chocolate sauces.

I'm not one for fancy desserts, but even *I* thought they were delicious.

Maybe it was because of the vanilla ice cream.

"Ready to hit the road?" Rosa asked when we were leaving the restaurant.

"I'm ready for another nap," I said.

Rosa laughed.

"Well, everything's packed up and in the

Mercy

truck," she said.

"I know," I said. "I was only kidding."

She smiled.

"Okay, then. I guess I'll follow you."

I hadn't thought about that.

I forget that Rosa had a car. Well, I didn't forget that she had a car. I just forget that we had to bring it.

"That's not fun," I said.

"Moving rarely is," Rosa said.

"How about if I get a trailer for your car, and you and I ride in the truck together?" I asked.

"Now *that* would make moving fun!"

So that's what we did.

Chapter 10

The ride back to Peaceville was great.

We talked and laughed the entire way.

At one point, my phone rang, and I saw it was Patti.

I didn't take the call, and then shut off my cell phone.

I didn't want anyone or anything to bother us.

I knew it would be a long time, if ever, that Rosa and I would have this kind of quality time together.

I know what you are thinking.

Sitting in a big, noisy truck for hours on end?

Mercy

I doubt that was what most of you would think of as "quality" time.

Having Rosa all to myself was what I thought was "quality" time.

Once we got home, we would be surrounded by friends. So I would not get Rosa all to myself.

Plus, there was the election to prepare for. So again, we would have lots of other people around.

And let's not forget Patti. *And* her lawsuits.

That sure wasn't something I was looking forward to.

I had to admit, though, I was now glad that the truck wouldn't go more than fifty miles per hour.

It stretched out our time together.

All of a sudden, I didn't hate that truck any more.

In fact, I *loved* that truck.

Just me and Rosa, plodding along.

Alone together.

Talking and laughing.

Finding out about each other.

She told me such great stories about her

childhood.

I wished I'd had such great stories, but I didn't.

My childhood was kind of bland.

But Rosa's childhood was filled with the love of her parents.

I'd figured out that her father was a great man at his funeral.

People had said such nice things about him.

He had helped so many people have better lives.

But her mother was also an amazing woman. And I loved hearing the stories Rosa told of the warm-hearted woman who brought her into this world.

I secretly thanked her mother for having Rosa. Because without her mother and father, Rosa wouldn't exist.

So I owed those two people a huge thank you.

I wished I could have met them.

But you can't change time.

They had both passed away.

Mercy

But I knew they would both be very proud of Rosa.

She was a good woman.

And she was raised right.

Her parents had taught her what was important.

I looked over at Rosa as she told me a story about when she was ten years old.

It was a funny story, and her eyes were sparkling with merriment.

For a moment I wished we never had to leave this old truck.

I realized that this trip was the closest thing to heaven I'd gone through in a long time.

Chapter 11

But like they say, "All good things must come to an end."

And we finally got to Peaceville.

I'd forgotten about small town living.

Everyone was gathered at Rosa's house.

It looked like they were having a ticker-tape parade for us.

It was really kind of nice.

And Rosa sure felt welcome.

Sure, I was a little upset that our time together was over.

But how selfish could I be?!

Mercy

Of *course* everyone else wanted to see her too.

The weird thing was that there were TV people there, too.

And they each had a camera crew.

Rosa tugged on my t-shirt.

She motioned for me to bend down to her.

I bent down and put my ear close to her mouth.

"And so it begins," she said.

Then I think she kissed my ear. But I wasn't sure. It happened so fast.

"So. Rosa. How's the race for sheriff going?" one TV person asked.

She was looking at the camera, not at Rosa.

But then the camera moved to point at Rosa.

"Well," Rosa said. "As you can see, we *just* got back to Peaceville."

Rosa pointed to the truck.

"***Welcome home***," someone shouted from the crowd.

Rosa laughed.

"**Thank you**," she shouted toward the crowd.

"*Are you coming to my Mom's party?*" the voice shouted back to Rosa.

That's when she realized that it was Rico.

Rosa's face lit up and she turned to me.

"That's Rico Vega," she said with a big smile.

"The Rico Vega you got released from prison?" one of the TV folks asked.

"The Rico Vega who was falsely accused of murder?" another TV person asked.

"That's the one," Rosa said.

Then she winked at me.

The TV crews rushed toward the crowd of people.

"Where is Rico Vega?" one of the TV people asked into the crowd.

"Come on," Rosa said. "Let's go."

She grabbed my hand and rushed me into her father's house.

She closed the front door and leaned on it.

"You can expect this kind of thing from here on out," Rosa said. "Until the end of the election."

Mercy

"Really?!" I asked.

Rosa nodded.

"The election for sheriff is big news around here," she said.

"So it looks like I'll get even *less* time alone with you," I said.

She hugged me and looked up at me.

"For a while," she said.

I kissed the tip of her nose.

"Thank you for helping me move, Dan," she said.

"It was my pleasure," I said. "Plus, it brought you home."

"It feels good to be home in Peaceville. Like I belong here."

"Funny," I said. "But that's how I feel, too."

"Like you belong here in Peaceville?" she asked.

"Well, yes. But also that *you* belong here in Peaceville. *With* me."

She leaned up on her tip toes and kissed me.

Of course that's when we heard Bubba.

Chapter 12

"Would you two, knock it off?! I'm trying to eat here!"

He strolled out of Rosa's father's kitchen.

"What are *you* doing in this house?!" I hollered at Bubba.

I think I was a little frustrated.

"The same thing *we're* doing here," Mel said.

"**Surprise!**" Henry, Hilda and Judge Simpkins said at the same time.

Yup. It was going to be a *long* time before Rosa and I had some time alone together.

I looked at Rosa.

Mercy

She grinned and shrugged.

I had to admit, *any* amount of time would feel like a long time.

But it was good to see our friends showing her such support.

"Look, you guys must be tired," Judge Simpkins said.

Rosa and I both nodded.

"So I cooked us some food," Hilda said. "Let's eat."

"And then someone can drive Dan home," Henry said.

"I was going to unload the truck," Dan said.

"We'll all come back in the morning, and will do it then," Mel said.

"With this many hands, we'll make short work of it," Henry added.

"So you won't need me, right?" Bubba asked.

Hilda threw a wet sponge at Bubba.

"We don't *want* you," she said.

"But we *need* you," Judge Simpkins said.

"So we're stuck with you," Mel finished.

Everyone laughed. Including Bubba.

"Sure, since you *need* me," Bubba said. "In the morning, I'll be back."

"He keeps coming back," Henry muttered.

"Like a bad penny!" Hilda said.

Then she cackled loudly.

"Let's eat, all!" she said as she waddled toward Rosa's father's kitchen.

Bubba threw the wet sponge back at Hilda.

It landed right on her wide bottom.

"Don't be fresh, young man! Or there will be no food for you!"

With that, Hilda cackled her head off.

Chapter 13

Henry drove me back to the junkyard.

"Mel is so excited to have Rosa home," he said.

I nodded.

"You are too, aren't you," Henry noted.

"Yes," I admitted. "I just wish I had more alone time with her."

"After the election, you will have more time together. Patience, my friend. Patience."

I smiled with my next thought.

"I keep having the same feeling," I said. "*So close and yet so far.*"

"I can understand that," Henry said.

Then Henry turned to me.

"What's going to happen with that lawsuit?" he asked.

"I have no idea," I said.

"Do you think there's a way you can talk Patti out of it?"

"I don't know," I said honestly.

"You know, a part of me thinks that she's doing this for leverage."

"Leverage?" I asked.

"I think she's figured out that you will protect your friends. So she will use that to make you do what she wants you to do."

"You think she's that conniving?" I asked.

Henry shrugged.

"I don't know her all that well. But maybe she is," he said.

I had to shake my head.

I turned to Henry.

"What did I ever see in her?" I asked him.

"Many men go for looks. Maybe that was all

Mercy

you saw."

"Maybe," I admitted. "But I must admit, I sure am embarrassed now."

Henry laughed.

"Well, you couldn't have been *too* off-base. *Bubba* thinks she's amazing, and she's *suing* him."

I had to laugh.

"There's no accounting for taste," I said.

Henry laughed a hearty laugh.

"I guess not," he said.

Chapter 14

I got home and fed the animals.

Bubba had been feeding everyone while I was gone.

Lucky looked happy to see me. So did the other dogs.

The cats didn't seem as if they cared.

But I knew they were just faking it. Trying to act cool.

A few had run up to me and walked by me, leaning their bodies against me as they passed.

That was as close to a cat hug as you could get.

Mercy

"Glad I'm home?" I asked Lucky.

I think he nodded.

"And I brought Rosa with me too," I said.

His tail wagged like crazy.

I really do think he understood me.

After I gave a pat to each animal, I went inside.

I crashed into bed and slept through to the morning.

I woke up refreshed and happy.

I was going to see Rosa today. And, hopefully, every day from here on out.

As planned, I met everyone at Hilda's.

We had breakfast together, and then unpacked the truck.

We helped Rosa put her stuff in her father's house.

"I guess we should stop calling it that," Mel had said at one point. "We should just call it *your* house."

Rosa nodded quickly. A tear welled up in her eye.

"This kind of reminds me that he's really gone," she said.

Mel went to hug Rosa.

I wished I would have gotten there first.

I wanted to hold her and comfort her.

Mel must have known that, because she motioned for me to join them.

We had a group hug.

Rosa cried a little, and clung to us.

"It's so good to be home," she said. "I just kind of wish Dad was here too."

"Me too," Mel said.

I had nothing to say, so I said nothing.

We broke apart shortly after that, and got back to work.

Rosa's things were now scattered in with her father's things. It looked nice. Homey.

She took over the master bedroom, and rebuilt the beautiful bedroom with her own stuff.

We hung up her curtains, and made the bed with her bedspread and pillows.

The lamps were placed on her night tables, and

Mercy

her dresser was centered on the far wall.

We put her parents' stuff in empty boxes.

Then we put those boxes in the truck.

We also moved Rosa's parents' old bedroom furniture to the truck so I could bring it to Goodwill.

Henry, Bubba and I went to Goodwill to drop off the stuff.

Then we dropped off the truck and the car trailer, back at the rental place.

By the time we got back to Rosa's house, it was time for all of us to go home and wash up for the party at the Vega's house.

Chapter 15

It was a great party!

Everyone was there.

We all brought something, so the party was not too big a burden on Mrs. Vega.

Mel brought her homemade organic salsa and chips and some mini tacos.

Rosa brought a few cases of soda and some paper plates and napkins.

Hilda brought cakes and pies and cupcakes.

Judge Simpkins brought enough baked beans for the entire town.

I had to take the old pickup truck because I

Mercy

brought my grill.

I also brought some hamburgers, hot dogs, and about four dozen buns. Two dozen hamburger buns and two dozen hot dog buns.

Bubba brought himself.

That was it.

Just himself and his appetite.

Jason Atkins was there.

He thanked Rosa for helping him clear his name.

"You need to give up your life of crime," Rosa told him.

He grinned.

"Are you saying that because you are running for sheriff?" he asked her.

"No," she said. "I'm saying that because you're not good at it. At all!"

Judge Simpkins and I started laughing.

But no one else got the joke.

So Rosa told everyone about Jason's crime spree.

"Here's just one of Jason's episodes," Rosa

told everyone.

The entire party got quiet.

"He broke into a *very* rich man's house. The man had multi-million-dollar paintings. He also had Fabergé eggs worth millions. But did Jason take any of *those*?" Rosa asked.

The crowd all said, "Noooooooo," at the same time.

"You are right," Rosa said. "He did not take any of those. He took the little knick-knack that the man's granddaughter bought at the dollar store!"

The crowd exploded with laughter.

Jason's face reddened.

"Don't you all think he should give up his life of crime?" Rosa said loudly to the crowd.

The crowd roared a raucous "YES!"

Then, when things died down a little, LaMont came over to speak with us.

"I want to thank you both," he said to us.

I let Rosa answer him. After all, if it weren't for her, he wouldn't be out of jail.

Mercy

I was just along for the ride while Rosa investigated and solved the whole serial killer thing.

"The state is giving me some money," he said. "Because the sheriff set me up and I would have rotted in jail if it hadn't been for you guys."

Rosa smiled at LaMont.

"I'm glad we could help," she said simply.

"Anyhow, with that money, I'm going to start my own A/C business. And I want to give you guys free A/C service. For life! Because that's how long I would have been sitting in prison."

Of course Bubba showed up at that moment.

"I helped," Bubba said. "Do I get free air conditioner service for life, too?"

"No," LaMont said quickly.

To be fair, I needed to say something.

"He really *did* help," I said. "*He's* the one who broke the knife, and *he* knew the sheriff's car on the video tape. In his own clumsy way, *he* was a big help in solving the case."

LaMont looked at Bubba.

"Well, okay," LaMont said. "I'll give you free A/C service. But only for your garage. Not for where you live. But in exchange, will you be my mechanic for my fleet of vans? And I only have to pay for parts?"

Bubba thought about that offer.

"How big is your fleet?" Bubba asked LaMont.

LaMont grinned.

"Right now? One. But I hope it'll grow."

"When you get more than three vans, will you give me free A/C service on my house too?" Bubba asked.

"Sure," LaMont said.

"You have a deal," Bubba said.

Then Bubba turned toward us.

"You heard that deal, right?" he asked us.

"Yes, but we noticed that you didn't tell LaMont that you might not have your garage for long," Rosa said.

"What?!" LaMont said. "You're *already* stiffin' me?!"

Mercy

"Don't worry," Bubba said. "It's a minor problem."

"You're losing your garage and you think that's a 'minor' problem?!" LaMont shouted.

"First of all," Bubba said. "I don't need a garage to fix your vans. I can fix your vans anywhere. You know I'm that good, LaMont."

LaMont had to agree with that.

"And second of all, Dan here's going to fix that whole problem for me. He's going to make it all go away. Right, Dan?"

"I'll *try*," I said. "But I can't make any promises."

Bubba turned to LaMont.

"Dan's got an in with the hottie who's suing me," he said with a grin.

LaMont stared at Bubba.

"Let me get this straight, Bubba. You've got the hots for the person who's *suing* you?! You are one crazy white boy!" LaMont said.

Then he laughed his head off.

Chapter 16

The party was great, and we all had a great time.

But then my phone rang.

It was Patti.

I was afraid not to take it. I didn't want to make her angrier than she already was.

She would take her anger out on Bubba. *And* the town.

"Dan? Please. Can we meet?"

"Are you out of the hospital?" I asked.

"I can check myself out," she said.

"I don't think that's a good idea, Patti. They

Mercy

wouldn't keep you in there if you didn't need to be there."

"This little po-dunk hospital?! They don't know *what* they are doing! Thank *God* this is nothing serious."

I had to ask.

"If it's nothing serious, Patti, then why are you suing Bubba and the town?"

She huffed, like she was tired of having to explain things to an idiot.

"Because they deserve it! What, does he think it's *funny* to keep rotten sandwiches in his vending machine? Who's laughing *now*, huh?"

Then she muttered under her breath.

"I'll show that freaky Goth pervert who he can and can't mess with!"

Then her whole demeanor changed.

"But that's not why I'm calling," she said almost sweetly.

I said nothing.

"I'd like for us to meet somewhere," she said. "So we can, um, talk."

The woman didn't get a hint.

I know she despised Bubba, just from his looks. But she had more in common with him than she knew.

They were both stubborn.

And neither one of them could take a hint.

"Please?" she begged.

I didn't answer.

Rosa was standing next to me.

"Is that Patti?" she whispered.

"Yes," I whispered back.

"What does she want?" Rosa whispered.

"To meet with me," I whispered back.

Rosa looked over at Bubba.

"So do it," she whispered.

"You think it's a good idea?" I whispered to Rosa.

"No," she whispered back. "But it needs to be done."

I nodded at Rosa.

"Okay," I said into the phone. "We can meet. Under one condition."

Mercy

"I'm listening," Patti said.

"You can't bad mouth my friends."

"Okay."

I gave Rosa the thumbs up.

She smiled and turned away to talk with someone.

I took three large steps away, so Rosa wouldn't hear what I said next.

"And you can't come on to me again," I said into the phone.

"You said *one* condition."

I rolled my eyes.

Yes, Patti and Bubba were a lot alike.

"Those are my conditions. Take them or leave them. It's your choice."

She sighed. "Okay, I'll take them."

"Repeat them," I said. Just in case she didn't get them.

"No bad mouthing the greasy Goth guy. No coming on to you."

I needed to clear things up a bit.

"You can't say anything bad about *any* of my

friends."

"You mean like the big, black, biker librarian? Or the old, cackling witch of a waitress?"

I didn't like the way she spoke of my friends.

It was best to keep Patti away from my friends. More for their sake, of course.

That's when it hit me. I really *did* love my friends and my new life.

"Okay," Patti said. "I'll play nice. I won't say anything about your friends. And I won't use my charms on you."

"Thank you," I said. Grateful for both.

"So what now?" she asked.

"I'll come by and get you from the hospital. We can talk at the yard."

"Okay," she said.

"I'll be there in fifteen minutes."

Chapter 17

Henry and Mel said that they would take Rosa back home from the party.

"Good luck," Rosa said as I said goodbye.

I nodded.

She looked a little worried.

I gave her a warm hug, and kissed her forehead.

"There's nothing to worry about," I told her.

She looked up at me and smiled.

"Thanks," she said. "I needed to hear that."

I hugged her again, so she would be assured.

Then I drove to the hospital.

Patti was waiting.

She was all dressed up.

She was dressed okay for a night on the town in New York City. But she was over-dressed for Peaceville.

She wanted to take her car. So I drove her, in her car, to the junkyard.

I took her elbow and guided her to my living room.

She stopped and gasped.

Not a good gasp. A gasp of horror.

"Before you speak," I warned. "You should know that I like it. It's homey."

I had to give her credit. She said nothing.

But her eyes said it all.

She was disgusted. Appalled.

She sat down gingerly.

I could tell she didn't want her skin to touch the fabric of the chair.

I tried not to roll my eyes.

"Dan," she said. "You can't possibly like living like this."

Mercy

"I do," I said. "And there's nothing wrong with my home."

"It's a... junkyard."

"So?"

"So. It's not a home."

"It *is*. And it's *my* home."

"Don't you want to come back home? To New York?"

"No."

"What about our friends?"

"They were *your* friends."

"Your job?" she asked.

"I quit."

"They'll take you back."

I thought about that last call to my boss.

"I doubt it."

"I called them," she said. "They want you back."

"You had no right!" I said. "Plus, I don't want to go back."

"You're being silly, Dan."

"No, I'm not."

"What about the theater? The night life?"

"I have a DVR, if I want to see something."

She made a face.

"What about the food? Don't you miss dining in five-star restaurants?"

I thought of Hilda's diner.

"No. Not one bit."

"What about the culture of New York?"

"There's plenty of culture here."

She made a face. It said, "I beg to differ."

"Don't you miss the country club?" she asked.

"That, least of all."

Her "convincing" came to a screeching halt.

"I can't think of anything else," she said to herself.

"So are we done here?"

"No," she said.

Her eyes looked desperate.

She needed to find something. *Anything*.

Her face lit up with her next thought.

"What about the money?" she asked.

"What money?"

Mercy

"All the money we had."

"You took it. Remember?"

"Well, yes. But didn't you like *having* it?"

I shrugged. "I thought I did."

"Well, you could have that again!" she said with glee.

"Why? Are you giving it back?"

Her face froze. All glee was gone.

"Well, no. We spent it all."

"We?" I asked.

"Neil and I," she said. "Mostly Neil."

"Uh huh," I said drily.

"But you could work and get it all back again," she said with excitement.

Her eyes were wide with promise, and hope.

But she wasn't speaking to a child.

And she wasn't speaking to a man under her spell anymore.

"I *could*," I said slowly.

She all but lit up like a Christmas tree.

She jumped out of her chair and clapped her hands.

"This is *great*!" she said.

I shook my head.

"I said that I *could*. But I didn't say that I *would*," I said with a little grin.

Her face dropped.

I wasn't trying to be mean. I was just trying to let her down easy. Sort of *ease* her into the fact that the golden goose was gone. Flew the coop. Down to Florida. To a junkyard.

"What does that mean?!" she demanded.

"It means that he's not your errand boy anymore," Bubba said as he came in.

"Or your human ATM," Rosa added.

"Or your cash register," Mel said.

"Or your whipping boy," Henry finished.

Patti was furious!

"How *dare* you!" she spat out.

She looked at me.

Most likely to see if I'd defend her.

I thought I'd help her out a little.

"Yes, Patti. That's kind of what that means."

She was shocked and insulted.

Chapter 18

Patti looked at my friends with contempt.

"I'm going to sue this town for every penny they've got!" she said.

"Well," Bubba said. "That's why we're here."

"To beg?" Patti said with scorn. "Believe me. That won't work on *me*!"

"Sorry, young lady," Judge Simpkins said. "We're not here to beg."

"And who are *you*?!" Patti asked the short, plump man with the round spectacles.

"That doesn't matter," the judge said.

"Yeah," Bubba said. "We're just here to tell

you that your lawsuit's been thrown out of court."

Patti looked confused.

"You made the dumb mistake of saying this..."

Bubba took out an MP3 player.

He pressed a few buttons and Patti's voice came through loud and clear.

"*This little po-dunk hospital?! They don't know what they are doing! Thank* God *this is nothing serious.*"

Bubba pressed another button.

"*Thank* God *this is nothing serious.*"

He pressed it again.

"*Thank* God *this is nothing serious.*"

"Want to hear it again?" Bubba asked.

"*Thank* God *this is nothing serious.*"

"How about one more time?" Bubba said.

"*Thank* God *this is nothing serious.*"

"This recording was made by a nurse. She was in your room. You didn't even *notice* that she was there," Bubba said.

"She sent it to the judge who was assigned the

case," Rosa said.

"And *he* threw the case out of court," the rotund, bespectacled man said with a twinkle in his eye.

Patti stormed out of the room.

Her high-heels clicking as she crossed the room to leave.

She tried to slam the screen door as she left, but it didn't work out very well for her.

We could also hear Lucky growl at her as she stomped to her little Lotus Elise.

Of course, we heard the tires squeal as she peeled out.

"That *really* ruins a good pair of tires," Bubba said.

"I know!" I said with a laugh.

Chapter 19

The days after that were anything but calm.

Sure, Patti was gone, but Carl Taggart had taken her place.

That man that had told me to be careful of him was right.

Carl Taggart was one mean guy!

He really didn't have any qualms about slinging mud.

He said things about Rosa that were *totally* untrue!

We didn't know where he was getting this stuff.

Mercy

Then we figured it out.

He was making it all up!

He left it up to us to either prove him wrong or ignore it.

He also knew we had no way of proving him wrong.

Mostly because the stuff he said had never happened to *begin* with!

How do you prove that nothing ever happened?!

You can't!

And Carl Taggart knew that!

He really was one wily fox. And not a nice guy at all.

Certainly not the kind of guy folks would want for sheriff. But how could *they* know?!

Carl Taggart was slinging so many lies, we couldn't keep up with them.

At one point, Rosa wanted to give up. She wanted to quit the race and be left alone.

The things Carl Taggart was saying were embarrassing.

He said that she slept around.

How do you prove that she *doesn't* do that?

He said she had loose morals, and showed pictures of me hugging her, Henry hugging her and Bubba hugging her.

We knew that we were all friends and that those hugs were innocent.

But the *people* didn't know!

Then Carl Taggart stated that the picture with Henry was of her doing something improper with a married man.

Talk about a smear campaign!

Sure, Henry was married. But he was only welcoming Rosa home. I was right there.

A reporter or someone took those pictures through the windows the night we'd moved Rosa back home.

They even posted a picture of Rosa and Mel hugging, implying that Rosa might also be a lesbian. *And* with the wife of the black man in the *other* picture.

They made Rosa sound like a perp you would

Mercy

see on Law & Order, SVU.

The sad thing was that none of it was true! At all!

So how do you fight that?!

The judge told us not to say a word.

Not to negate anything.

Not to put gas on the flames.

He told us to say nothing.

He told us to ignore it all.

But that was hard to do.

I wanted to defend Rosa.

She wanted to defend herself.

But we took the judge's advice.

We figured that if the people didn't want Rosa to be sheriff, then so be it.

Chapter 20

It had been a long few weeks.

Once the election was over, I finally had some time to think about all that had happened the last couple months.

I needed to reflect. To learn something from what had happened.

My mind went back to Patti.

"Bubba?" I asked.

"Yeah, boss?"

"Do you think I was a wuss when I was married to Patti? You know, for letting her walk all over me?" I asked. "And stop calling me boss."

Mercy

Bubba looked right at me.

"Nah. I would have let that woman do anything to me. *Anything*!" he said with a big wink.

"I just needed to answer to my own idea of what type of man I wanted to be. I've always wanted to be a good man."

"You *are* a good man, Dan," Bubba said. "And we all make a good team. You and me and Rosa and Henry and Mel and Hilda and the judge. I was afraid you were going to run off with Patti. Now that you're here, you *can't* leave."

I looked at Bubba. "Why not?"

"It would be like when Grissom left CSI. Things just wouldn't be the same," Bubba said.

Miles walked through the door.

"Hey all," he said.

"Hey, Miles," Bubba and I said together.

"Good to see you again, my friend," I said to Miles.

"You too, Dan," Miles said.

It had been a while since we had seen Miles. I still didn't know where he went when he left the junkyard, but it didn't matter.

I was just glad he was back.

And he looked good.

"I hear Rosa won. That's so great! I heard it was a real smear campaign," Miles said.

"You have no idea," Bubba said. "But the judge wouldn't let us fight back."

Miles thought about that.

"No, you did the right thing. *All* of you did the right thing. I heard you, Dan, showed mercy on Patti. And I heard that *all* of you showed mercy on Carl Taggart. You took the high road. I'm proud of all of you."

Bubba snorted a laugh.

"It was tough!" Bubba said.

Miles nodded.

"Showing mercy always is," Miles said. "It's said that the mark of a *true* warrior is mercy."

I thought about that, and liked that I could honestly say that I had taken that path.

Mercy

Read the *next* book of the
Junkyard Dan
series
to find out what's going on with
Dan, Rosa, Bubba,
Henry, Mel, Hilda,
Judge Simpkins and Miles.

If you are enjoying the

Junkyard Dan

series,
we have a few **other** series
that you might *also* like to
read...

Want comedies?

Try reading...

THE
SMITH
BROTHERS

Come meet Les, Ling, Luiz and Bob.
They **are** "The Smith Brothers."

(And they're *completely* insane!)

NOX PRESS
books for that extra kick to give you more power
www.NoxPress.com

Everyone has it
within them
to be a

Do **you**?

NOX PRESS
books for that extra kick to give you more power
www.NoxPress.com

The

LEADER

series.

HONOR
COURAGE
RESPECT
SERVICE
INTEGRITY
COMMITMENT
LOYALTY
DUTY

(We bet you can't read just one!)

HUNGER FOR ACTION?

Welcome to

Pete drives a lunch truck.

He's a nice enough guy,
but there's something about him
that makes his customers wonder.

And what's with the bullet holes
all over the truck?!

NOX PRESS
books for that extra kick to give you more power
www.NoxPress.com

We also have
a funny series called:

A LEEG OF HIS OWN

Andrew Leeg is one of a triplet. And the only boy.
So, as you've probably guessed,
the other two are girls.
Yeah, that's right. Two sisters.
Abbie Leeg and Annie Leeg.
They always bug Andrew.
And nag him like you would *not* believe!
It's always two against one. And usually, the girls win.
But Andrew always goes down fighting!
He's *truly* in...

NOX PRESS
books for that extra kick to give you more power
www.NoxPress.com

Want to read more NOX PRESS books?

Go online to
www.NoxPress.com
to see what's being released!

Books can easily be purchased online or you can contact **Nox Press** via the Website for quantity discounts.

Are you a fan?

Do you want us to put *your* comments up on our Website?

If so, please e-mail them to:
NoxPress@gmail.com

NOX PRESS
books for that extra kick to give you more power
www.NoxPress.com